One Glad Man

Written by
Lynea Bowdish

Illustrated by
Kristin Sorra

Rookie
reader®

Children's Press ®
A Division of Grolier Publishing
New York • London • Hong Kong • Sydney
Danbury, Connecticut

For Mitch Augarten—listener, supporter, friend.
—L. B.

Reading Consultants

Linda Cornwell
Coordinator of School Quality and Professional Improvement
(Indiana State Teachers Association)

Katharine A. Kane
Education Consultant
(Retired, San Diego County Office of Education
and San Diego State University)

Visit Children's Press® on the Internet at:
http://publishing.grolier.com

Library of Congress Cataloging-in-Publication Data
Bowdish, Lynea.
     One glad man / written by Lynea Bowdish ; illustrated by Kristin Sorra.
        p. cm.—(Rookie reader)
     Summary: Rhyming text describes the animals, from one to ten, that take up
residence in a lonely man's home.
     ISBN 0-516-21595-7 (lib. bdg.)   0-516-26545-8 (pbk.)
     [1. Counting. 2. Animals—Fiction. 3. Stories in rhyme.]
I. Sorra, Kristin, ill. II. Title. III. Series.
PZ8.3.B67250n 1999
[E]—dc21   98-53086
                                                              CIP
                                                              AC

One sad man . . .

. . . living all by himself.

Two brown ants
build a home on the shelf.

Three stray dogs
snuggle up in the chairs.

11

Four gray cats
move in under the stairs.

13

**Five bright bees
make a hive on the ledge.**

Six fat worms
set up house near the hedge.

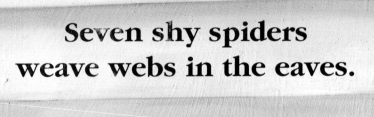

Seven shy spiders
weave webs in the eaves.

Eight small birds
hide their nests in the leaves.

Nine nice mice
curl up under the floor.

Ten green frogs
come to play by the door.

One glad man,

he's not sad and alone.

29

All his new friends
are now sharing his home.

WORD LIST (78 words)

a	dogs	himself	nice	spiders
all	door	his	nine	stairs
alone	eaves	hive	not	stray
and	eight	home	now	ten
ants	fat	house	on	the
are	five	in	one	their
bees	floor	leaves	play	three
birds	four	ledge	sad	to
bright	friends	living	set	two
brown	frogs	make	seven	under
build	glad	man	sharing	up
by	gray	mice	shelf	weave
cats	green	move	shy	webs
chairs	he's	near	six	worms
come	hedge	nests	small	
curl	hide	new	snuggle	

About the Author

Lynea Bowdish and her husband, David Roberts, live with two dogs, one goldfish, and all of the friends mentioned in *One Glad Man*, except the cats. She grew up in Brooklyn, New York, where she first started to write, and now lives in Hollywood, Maryland.

About the Illustrator

Born and raised in Baltimore, Maryland, Kristin Sorra grew up with a passion for art and telling stories. So she pursued her interest and studied illustration at Pratt Institute in Brooklyn, New York. Kristin currently resides in Brooklyn with her husband. *One Glad Man* is her first book.